Emergency Press International Book Contest

There, Heather Rounds

Selected by Ewa Chrusciel

THERE

HEATHER ROUNDS

Emergency Press
New York

Design by Lindsay Gatz/Artsy Geek
Cover photograph by the author

Rounds, Heather
There
ISBN 978-0-9836932-8-4
1. Fiction—General. 2. Fiction—Literary. 3. Fiction—Travel

Emergency Press
154 W. 27th St.
#5W
New York NY 10001
emergencypress.org

987654321
First Printing

Printed in the United States of America
Distributed by Publishers Group West

THERE
A NOVEL

HEATHER ROUNDS

AUTHOR'S NOTE

This book consists of events, incidents, sentences formed
from Moleskine notes, anecdotes, oral histories, people—
all of it carried a far distance. In some ways, alterations
have intentionally been written in, out of respect for those
involved. In other ways changes have occurred naturally—in
that way recollection lives on, separate from experience.

"If a lion could talk, we could not understand him."

—Wittgenstein's *Philosophical Investigations*

I

KANIN:
TO PULL UP, UPROOT, DIG

Friday in thick August heat, the holy day of rest, the result of an online classified ad. Everything around her now ticks to a stop. Distant, limp trees on dry plains and the foothills lining the city blur in haze. A giant yellow generator vibrates, next to a small white trailer, where two guards—barely 18, barely heavier than their kalishnakoffs—sleep away the afternoon. For now, it's new. No bitter dust storm battles the clouds, blackbirds aren't yet buzzards, the dog has yet to thump by tied to a moped.

The young Kurdish woman, four yards down, pinning laundry and banging rugs against cinders, spots her, breaks the quiet—

My home. Go my home, come!

Running from her yard, the Kurdish woman takes her arm. And then the woman's husband in his white muddy pick-up. Come, he echoes his wife, a torso stretched through the window.

She goes. Up to their small apartment, warm and doll-like. The young woman parts the heavy red curtains, waking the man asleep on the floor, kicks him toward another room.

Here-here-here-sit, the Kurdish husband sings, pointing to the corner—a window spot, a pinkish cushion, some stray black seeds, maybe watermelon, and something grainy, maybe sugar, caught in the stitching.

She offers them the Kurdish word for thank-you. In return they give her a Kurdish phrase that translates as *on your eyes!* She knows this means *your welcome!* She has nothing more than this. From them she can take nothing more than this. Blackbirds pass, just beyond the window.

She'd said Iraqi Kurdistan and Everyone asked, *Why go there?*

Because. Why go elsewhere?

Because. She decided to think things were possible, despite anything and everything she knew. The word *possible* nuzzled, nipped, until a hole began and crawled through to where, over twenty some years, she'd slowly gone buried under herself. Not a peek of light anywhere. The word *possible* came to break it all up, throw her out, show her stuff. Because she answered the online ad and two weeks later the Kurdish Regional Government offered a year-long contract as an editor and journalist at their English-language newspaper. Because they needed someone who spoke and wrote in English. Because she needed money and could make decisions fast. Because she believed her resume was weaker than she was. Because the paper was government funded—a safe, secure job with a translator and driver, free accommodations in a guarded and spacious villa. Because it was Northern Iraq, Iraqi Kurdistan, the Land of the Kurds, the Cradle of Civilization, The Other Iraq. *Because you will fall in love with it here.*

Ask about them and she'd say they're okay—the two other women in this guarded and spacious villa. English teachers, and just as new: O from North Britain, putty arms, shifting bags of duty free Marlboros, toppled Absolute Vodka. Y from Boston, Louis Vuitton luggage, a delicate voice that calls home daily, candy-colored everything.

Their villa sits at the lip of an arid valley, near a sandbagged checkpoint, inside the alloy fence line, close to the USAID compound, a Lebanese import and trade company, Chinese engineering company, oil-this-and-that company, land mine removal organization, two Australian private security agencies, three Lebanese-owned bars, a roadside petrol stand, and several other villas, all in varying stages of completion, all in varying states of guarded.

Kurdistan's long, coarse cough, roots down, rattles deep, shoots up the torso, bleeds off flares like a sparkler, snags the throat, fragments the mouth, and nose. Just four days and it takes these three women. But it gives them something to say, some communal point among the sprouts of their difference. It takes them, this cough, the congestion of dust and generator exhaust, every time they push open or pull closed the villa's iron gate.

CHONI: HOW ARE YOU?

Not most, but some Kurdish restaurants consist of slippery objects—large creamy tiles and mustard velvet chairs—and unaffordable food, bright foods like salads and star shaped fruits. This one includes a pink-lit waterfall and no patrons other than her and the rest of the newspaper: six chain smoking men in suits of various browns and greens, hair slick and black, tea severely slurped, a masculine, acrid smell hovers, a welcome dinner. Only the editor-in-chief has words.

No one can afford it now, true, but that will change, he says, poking a forked cherry tomato in the vacant air, looking nothing like she had imagined.

He says *this will be the next Dubai. Someday I hope there will be a disco in a place like this. This place could hold a disco. This country wants to change. Soon there will be shopping malls and helicopter pads on the roofs of hotels. They are building them now. Progressive. We are progressive enough to have you here. It's not by chance that you are American. Everyone back home should be proud of you.*

He slips fast between languages and topics, mechanical. His posed questions outweighing any answers. He's the sort with a pompadour, the sort who went to *uni in Sweden*, the sort with a driver in sharkskin pants.

There are lots of opportunities for you in this region. Here, you can have it all, really, and you will—you will see, he tells her, spreading her conclusions all over the table, nimble and light as cards.

She takes it politely, a nod and a smile, some simple chirped
words that quickly removed themselves from the scene.
Clearly, her words aren't expected tonight and that's fine.
A week here and she can't shake this tired. Everything feels
giant.

Giant. Walking out the restaurant doors. The golden ticks
of a distant trash fire, the smell of paper burning and
singing—the shrill sounds from the throats of invisible
women beyond the fence line.

(Everyone: Most would never remember which *stan*. Some expected she'd come back decapitated. Regardless they admitted—mostly while drunk and far into another time— that yes they'd felt proud. None of it will matter.)

The editor-in-chief would rather start her editing the stories of the others.

Until you feel at home to write your own stories, he says, a large, stiff smile.

So she edits—fixes their words, swaps them out for others, rearranges, respells, alters fragments. It falls into place quick in this smoky box of an office, six days a week and into the nights. 3 computers, 1 couch, a TV flashing Swedish videos and streams of English Aljazeera. Sometimes as they speak, she adds details they lack. They resent this, or so she assumes by the way they swerve from English to Kurdish, the heavy pauses and changing of topics when her questions come, sometimes forgetting she exists for most of the day. But they like her, she assumes, too—judging by the constant tulip shaped glasses of tea that take up her desk, and the aggressive way they insist she take their cigarettes. And it will do.

WHAT'S NOT PREPARED FOR

Here. A dust storm comes with gristle in the bread, cigarette cellophane wrapped around the gate, a blue plastic bag affixed to the window. It's weakening her skin, thinning it ugly. She knows soon the bones will break through. Thorny in the bright dry day.

These tablets of expired Ibuprofen, imported from India, this hole in an old stonewall pharmacy, this leather lump man, haggling the price from 50 dollars to 1.

Insane. Another word to learn in Kurdish.

Eastern toilets. Hovering above the hole, knees over feet, facing forward, taking the plastic water can from the corner, either blue or salmon pink, tilting and hoping for water, cupping the water in the palm, splashing up and wiping, repeating as needed. (If and when possible, taking Kleenex, napkins, whatever might be scrounged. Throw in trash not down hole!)

An Aussie and a Lebanese, two villas down, here doing airport security. From the start they stay constant, somewhere between nuisance and sitcom, opening her door, refrigerator, their mouths, their spilled drinks sticking to her rooftop, taking over tables with their chewy piles of paper and wrappers.

Or, like tonight—Skye vodka and Dunhill cigarettes.

Y says, *no, would rather go to bed.* O says, *you're tired because you're too sober.*

Maybe.

We can change that.
Nope.

Y has a story about the time she drank out of the wrong 7-Up glass, but not now, another night.

(Ask Y why Kurdistan, and you'll hear about her uncle in Saudi Arabia, what he has to do with announcing Ramadan. Some administrative link between the moon's crescent, a month of fasting and how the Muslim world finds out it's time. How exactly, Y can't say, but she knows he's wealthy and keeps the king's number on speed dial. If you ask her what this has to do with Kurdistan, she'll respond, *actually nothing,* blushing, raking a candy pink nail over a hair wisp.)

Standing with the Aussie at the railing. She leans far until a head rush pulls her back. He spits into the dark below, tells her why he hates the Vietnamese. A sign to sleep, she thinks. Then the minaret—full-bellied, graceful, bending long with dawn's call to prayer.

Wow. It's morning. Yawning, his sour breath everywhere.

Yep. Out there, she says, nodding toward the orange crack shaping the city from blackness.

People have already driven places to sit on their knees and talk to God. People have already slept and woke and we

Edit. An essay about a poet who wrote about nights darker than his lover's hair. Poems more beautiful than death. A poet who once lived in prison, briefly in Sweden and most often in a tin-mud house. A poet who took a bullet in the mouth while walking through a park, protesting government oppression.

Her question squeezes them into their tea—maybe they've mistranslated.

More *beautiful* than death?

MAX

(as in *Mad Max*, named by the Aussie) has matted hair
and dirt gaunt cheeks, always seems drunk but not and
those who look close enough (no one other than her, she's
convinced) know. Catch him at the just-right time, he'll tell
you about anything. All the engineering degrees, how he
brought the water here, how he squeaks electricity from the
USAID compound's generators and pumps his TV up with
life, colors, how he built the TV, how he built the colors,
his bike, his cardboard walls, okra, wires and rafters, how he
lived midair to bring the water down, how he died during
war with Iran and went to Abu Ghraib, how he woke and
found himself here cooking French fries on Thursday nights,
how his English got so good.

Inside the villa, BBC reports a Turkish invasion could roll
in soon, north from the Qandils, where Turkey touches Iran
and Iraq. Again, the Turks against the PKK guerillas—the
armed struggle, the gutted-out rocks, the packed-in pistols.
Again with the shelling, collapsing mud brick, burning
valley orchards and black hide tents. Again the dulled-down
political traction, the blown-up bus, the caves of Chinese
rocket launchers and grenades. Again the displaced, villages
stinking with what remains behind. It could reach as far
as Erbil this time. It will reach her and Everybody would
have been right. Surely there'll evacuate, take precaution, the
USAID compound will close, the international school, too.
Evacuation. She sees herself and others, collected together,
stranded and sprawled over the airport lobby's carpet,
backpacks as pillows, coffee and card games, helpless as to
what's next or where. She thinks, Why not?

Invasion, evacuation, the Lebanese laughs, shaking some word-
grunts loose from his head, *not even close. For sure.*

(She sees the shame in her thoughts dragging through her.
Impossible to pin.)

WHAT'S SURE

Hair slumped and sweat lined, the young Kurdish woman in her yard, hangs her carpets, demands her new friend follow her inside. She should come in and stay, perhaps forever. Up the narrow stairwell, to the cushions, drink the tea and eat the watermelon, dinner and breakfast, inside the heavy red curtains, keeping it all out there.

She peeks through the curtains. It's all out there. Branching, out endless.

SURFACES TO BE CAREFUL WITH

Never above the knee, never much above the elbow, always at
the neck, never shake the hand, never show the soles of feet,
never alone with a man, don't dig too fast or it falls apart in
your hand.

Every fat, angry fly and mosquito in town. They knit her
face, waiting at the downtown taxi stand for O, who finally
comes, impossible to miss: a tank top, white pants, a sequin
buckle, a blonde head splitting the crowd.

Christ, they screech their tires enough with their stares as it
is, she says.

What's a stare mean, love?

The Edge: a bar at the USAID compound, open on
Thursday nights only. At the door, a khaki suit man checks
your passport. He says, *welcome to the Edge of Iraq*, then laughs,
pauses, waits for your giggle, and makes it clear with his
bobbing eyes, he'll wait as long as he needs to hear it. Inside,
a half-hooked dartboard dangles above blue Sharpie blurbs
like: *70 KM to Kirkuk. 80 KM to Mosul. Killer plus Bleep were
here.* Tonight, her first and only time at the Edge, she's one
of six women—O and Y, two Ethiopian prostitutes, and
going by the biceps and buzzed cut, probably a contractor,
Australian.

O figured it out, this room of men: thin, suited, older =
investors. Muscular, shaved heads = security contractors.

Y thinks it's sad you could break them all down into two
teams.

O dramatically rolls her eyes, says, *sure, we say that now after a
few weeks, love, but just give us another month.*

Across the room, the Lebanese holds his wrist atop the bar,
a lighter to it, proving his auburn band of prayer beads won't
burn.

This is how you prove they are real, he explains to the Ethiopians.
The real cannot be burned away.

Then Max from the kitchen, says he sees *something of this light*,
in the glint of the fork he holds, and the oily bubbles in the
French fry basket he drops at her table. He says, *look into that!*

A STAIRCASE WITH NO RAILS THAT LEADS TO A ROOM WITH NO CEILING

Some days off work, watching the half-finished house next door, smoking cigarettes on the roof—it takes up most of her. Leaves her bones thorny in the bright dry day.

The editor-in-chief gives her a driver and translator, says *now go find stories about our history and culture. The stories that could use a feminine voice. Stories about ancient relics or the kinds of flowers that grow in the mountains.*

Her driver has a thin face of bird-fine features, a voice like soft cracking branches. On their drives, he slips in between sighs just how much he hates his job. She apologizes awkwardly, unsure of what could be said instead, tightly gripping the seat, tossing the belt loop, a fit of tics.

The thing about me, says the driver, *is that I lived elsewhere, and I understand the difference between one freedom and another.*

(He has sparse stories of years spent in London with his wife, working at a box factory, long, shivering winters. She doesn't ask questions, but silently inflates the story—him in the warehouse, taping boxes, the cumbersome sounds of forklifts and box cutters, the world shutting down under the pressure of questions: *Am I where I should be?* His wife in their drafty kitchen, cooking dolma, maybe singing, bitter, hopeful, waiting for the key in the door.)

Her promised translator, AZ, shoots from all angles with severe gestures and statements—his words ballistic bodies, collecting momentum every time she asks for his help. He's spread so thin as it is he tells her, slamming a chewed up copy of *Leaves of Grass* on her desk.

I'm a student of Western literature, too, besides this.

She looks up to his wide, young face, severe copper eyes. She's bloated by a thousand questions, frustrations, but decides she likes him, gets him fast—the sharp of his angst, the way papers fly around him. Elsewhere and otherwise, they might have shared their adolescent poetry or drug habits or any number of passing trends at some other damage-prone age.

Her first article, first interview, goes wrong. The issue of limited textbooks at primary school 9. A blue-chipped paint, squat building, crinkling with papers of crayon sunshine. The school's teacher, barely twenty, gives off a burning smell of rosewater, her black eyes lined in an electric jade matching her headscarf.

She wants to like all Americans, *but it is hard—so hard, the way the soldiers kill. The way they kill children. I want to but it is so hard, with everything they are doing down there in Baghdad—my only true home. It is so hard, being forced north here. I should be a computer engineer, you know. That's my degree. We should keep smiles, you are too sensitive. I see in your eyes what I am saying makes you sad. To be here—you shouldn't be so sensitive. And how can you be here? How can you be so far away from your family? You are strong. It must be that you are strong. And you must be strong. I can tell you the story of when I was sad for two years, just after my breasts changed. This was when something happened to my period. Something happened and I was in love at university and I thought he loved me. The way he talked to me, I thought he loved me. But then I found out that he didn't love me, he loved my friend. And my friend was married. In my country she could have been killed. He shouldn't have done what he did—to love her. And I was sad for two years after this. Can you understand that story, no... you do, I see it in your eyes. I still don't understand why you wanted to come here. Why? You are too sensitive. They have a word in my language for girls like you who are too sensitive—*

She cuts the tangent, clicks off the recorder, not needing whatever descriptive word this woman has lodged in her and daylight's going fast through the thin door vents.

LOH? WHY?

Because of three memories, two years old now.

1: In Turkey with B. Turquoise water, granite ruins, bottled water-vodka. He climbed the wasted walls and she went dizzy knowing how easy he could fall. He'd jumped, to prove he could, swam far, fast, so far she lost sight of him, she couldn't chase him if she tried and fear ground her down in the granite. Then he reemerged, laughing, scraped her off the rock.

2: Last day of the trip, en-route to an airport, held up at a bus station, three sunk-faced kids on rice bags full of pots and clothing, up from Baghdad through Kurdistan and now here. B handed them the last two plums, they smirked and the father nodded thank-you. She fell in love with excitement, folded in on its brightness, tightly—a heavy gauge trap of happiness, fear—and inwardly acknowledged having no real knowing of the world.

And most of all 3: Because, two months later, when he broke it off, he said, *this is all there is* and spit out something of Nietzsche: *One should die proudly when it is no longer possible to live proudly.* But no one's dying, she said and it all came quick as a small white shock heading straight to the nerve, cutting the metallic smell of the bed sheets, the doughy rhythms of light coming through the window—the reflections of car mirrors, landing in their laps. The morning and everything before dissolved, endless empty, leaving only weighty white walls, dry clicking heat pipes, dust spinning mid-air, stupidity, stupidity, and a single tightly curled sound springing loose from her bed as he rose. His closing question: *What's possible?*

ERBIL IS ARBIL IS IRBIL IS SOMETIMES HEWLER OR HAWLER

Even the name of this city lacks consistency. Sometimes beginning with A or I or E, sometimes in clay and sometimes in steel.

It's difficult to edit. Difficult to edit and hot. Eye-pricking hot and creaking with metal hooks of hung snakes glistening black, splayed long-ways down the middle. Especially in the dense center, where air evaporates by noon, and watermelons under wool blankets in carts become hard to look at. And the crowd, and the coughs. Dust. Wires at every angle, sagging down on every street electric pole, thousands and thousands, sagging black blockage.

Today, some corner opens and out comes blue tattoos spiraling over a stretched out palm, a black headscarf tight over a small head and a voice like dropping gravel.

What the voice says can't be said but the palm is loud.

Between a star-shaped apple and a half-glass of ouzo, the editor-in-chief lets her know it's not just her, *it's just no one's been paid. The money's all tied up in Baghdad and they have bigger issues down there. Corruption, here, is not a moral issue. It's not a matter of right or wrong.*

AZ the translator, eye spark, earnest turn, clean pause, the near violent set down of his teacup.

Was it you who edited my title? Truly you must know why it worked there, the word whilst?

I avoid editing titles when I can, she says, her irritation peeking through.

And also, I wondered. . .where you are from, isn't it strange to not be married at your age?

Trees? The two stories explaining the absence of trees in Kurdistan, illustrate why her driver hates it here:

The Kurds hacked the woods themselves, for the sake of mountain bonfires.

It was Saddam and the Baathists—a tactic stripping the Kurds of all hiding places, any shield from bullets, sprays and chemicals.

Both true and both signs of fools, he says.

So, avoid doing tree stories, she says.

Fools! His word, a reptile tongue whip. A thin slap at her slumped frame.

She slumps further and the road spreads too quietly ahead.

ISHTAR WAS HERE

The ancient citadel, the original city, an abandoned clay fortress on a high dirt hill, sick cats, where the peshmerga soldiers slip to sleep, just past the rusty pile of sunflower oilcans and left of the blue-bronze gated bathhouse, a shanty corner of couches, armchairs, soldiers slugged under mildew carpets, smurf curtains, cockeyed rifles and trousers, inside the scalloped horizon of satellite dishes, an illusion of tight containment. The newspaper says, *make a story out of it.*

So far, she has the slack-eyed rug seller, saying he knows Ashurnazipal was here 900 years before Christ, and Nebuchadnezzar stole it from Sennacherib, and Darius from him, then came Alexander the Great, Mithridates and the Mongols, then Ishtar.

Confused, she asks, Ishtar lived here? The goddess?

Yes, of course (his eyes barely, and leaving) *they came here to pray at her feet for good battles.*

He knows because this is where his father was born—in a hole carved from the clay wall. He's not sure of much more, except he knows the ground would rise each time someone came and stole the city from someone else. The new king hung the flayed skin of the last on the wall, letting everyone below know a new city was crushing the last, countless times, piles upon piles, until no one could say what was.

If Ishtar lived here, shouldn't there be some sign? Like, a statue? She asks.

AZ says there are no facts. Don't look. Last year they forced everyone to leave, saying they would preserve it. Excavate and preserve it. But so far it is just an empty home for broken pieces. There are many worlds underneath us, but no one can be bothered to dig deep enough to find them. Not much story for you is what you're thinking I know, but think as the Romantics would. Think with intuition, no reason necessary. Think with what Wordsworth said: fill paper with what your heart breathes.

RASTA: GO RIGHT

She thought she'd left green eyes in America, but he has them—this acquaintance of an acquaintance back home. A Kurdish journalist of some independent, non-party paper, from the city of Suleimania. Sea glass eyes, green as washed out beer bottles, greener than any here or anywhere. He pulls up to the villa in a white Opal. Takes her to Ballentines, a Lebanese bar named after a Scottish whiskey, known for its framed beer posters of tube-topped Scandinavian blondes. It feels like home in all the wrong ways.

His advice: *Don't be concerned, dear, but people are going to stare. They are not used to seeing a face like yours. You must use this.*

You mean I should get used to it? She clarifies.

Of course.

She feels them. Men sucking lemons. Their words plop and slither on the table like chewed up gristle fat. She fights an urge to stare back, feels small and limbless.

Pistachio shells roll and lemons from their ouzos gum their elbows, conversations begin about politics, and journalism, about the difference between Lebanese and Iraqi dancing, spliced with missed segue ways, strategic segue ways, the precise and full silence of a mutual pause. He tells her about his trip to America, about hating the food and loneliness, about his brother's unrequited love for a Christian, the car he wrecked and the promise to his mother to become a safer driver, about wanting to return to journalism in Baghdad, about giving the white Opal back to his brother if his brother ever found a job, about the state of independent journalism in Kurdistan, government suppression, the woman's body just found stoned outside a village not so far away, the displaced villagers caught in the shelling on the Iranian and Turkish borders, the execution of his father. He's got stories about covering the Saddam trial, the Green Zone karaoke and endless buffets, the decline of his country, the ruling parties. He talks too much, but she generally listens. She listens while her eyes stray toward the Saudi Arabian pop videos fluttering from a dusty television bobbing from cables over the bar. She traces the contours of Arabian pop singers. Their almond butter hips and sharp arched brows. She generally listens and there's Arabian pop, the feral stares of men and her smallness. She listens and for every one thing she finds familiar here—endless, alien, inescapable things have her cornered. She's learning.

DIG IN BUT NOT TOO FAST OR IT FALLS APART IN YOUR HANDS

Don't keep a pattern when you walk—switch up your route. Keep a notepad for license plate numbers (suspicious cars, cars that slow down when they pass, etc.). Keep on the sidewalk when there is one. Inside by sunset. Never walk in large groups. Keep close—your breaths, your words, don't let it get too far from you.

The Kurdish woman crouches over a kitchen floor of white
onions and sinewy eggplants, the tangy steam of beef coats
the window.

Look close to this here.

The woman picks up an eggplant, takes a small knife,
sharply cuts away the tip, carves a circular divot with
two twists of the thumb and index. She hands it to her,
motioning her to hollow it out. But as the American turns
the knife, she digs in too fast and it falls apart in her hands.
The woman clicks her tongue and hands her another.

Slow.

First a small dent, a small hole, and move in deep, careful,
down through the center to bring up the meat, slow. But she
can't, she stabs through the skin and the Kurdish woman
laughs, as dinner gets snagged apart. She'd really truly like to
get it.

AMJA: NOW

What they thought was a bomb would turn out to be the victory of a soccer team. From the roof, first a white crack-crack-crack flash up the backs of geckos as they zip then the sudden bust of the guards from their trailer, a vodka and sprite gets tipped off the table.

Until this, nothing had been, beyond the story of an exploding generator. Until this, the guards had stayed sleepy. In the blankness between houses and into the dark dust and rubbish—now they snap awake and run.

LATIR: OUT OF THE CORNER OF ONE'S EYE

A chicken's foot, disintegrating on the hot concrete.

The acquaintance of an acquaintance raises the guards from the lawn chairs with his car. They circle, falling back as she opens the gate, opens the car door. He lets his words loose—

I cannot respect them. Dear, I am afraid I was not nice to them.

x

He takes her for dinner at a hotel called Four Lights. A soft lawn of cloth covered tables, air quilted with fat, ruddy, western cheeks, open-mouthed laughs, the clank of ice in glass, the heat of kabob and onions. As they're led to their table by a maitre d', she imagines they must look like a couple. It causes something to burrow between her legs. A throbbing.

At dinner, he orders for them—a platter of *mezzas*—and when she mistakes the *mezzas* for the dinner course, he corrects her, gives her three soft clicks of the tongue to show his joking disappointment. Turns out *mezza* isn't food, just what you eat while you drink. Her mistake makes him laugh. She takes it as a cue to laugh and laughs.

Maybe it's the tongue clicking, she can't say, but as they laugh she finds herself listening for something that might leave her wanting more. She waits for what's burrowed between her legs to find its way out and spread across the lush green lawn.

He continues talking, and as he does, her gaze drifts down
to her plate of rice and almonds. His words continue piling
and she realizes, looking up, an obstruction's appeared on
the table, cutting the view between them. The sound darkens,
too—his voice now that thinning echo where a tunnel opens.
His talking doesn't stop, just her ability to completely hear
the words.

And, so, it's confirmed on this night that nothing in his
voice, his green eyes, his anything, should leave her wanting
more. She tells herself just as well, better to leave this
relationship simple. She hasn't shaved in weeks.

x

The Man of Small Vital Facts is the nickname she gives him.
That's what he is: facts. Not so much small, or even vital—
but the kind that usually remain hidden in a place like this.
The kind that require effort to unearth. Facts. He says he
loves to reveal them, no matter what it means, be it jail
time, death threats, near misses when a white van bolts from
nowhere as he crosses the street. It's what it means to be a
true journalist in his country. It's the difference between his
country and hers, he says.

She will always keep the nickname to herself.

x

Entering the gates of Erbil Park, they get frisked at separate
stalls. The women—silk blankets of hair, sparkle-bead

necks, looped to men in shiny fabric suits—narrow their eyes on her. He buys two freezer burnt Nestlé ice cream cones and they walk along a man-made lake. As they walk, picking the aluminum wrappers from their ice creams, his talking wanes.

(Rare, but he does have pauses in him. Awkward, unpredictable pauses that cause his other traits to pop—his eyes brighter or his smell stronger. A fume smell, maybe propane.)

All things slow. Tree breeze, dinner whisky head, black pearl sky, the cadence of their walk. With the quiet, the ice cream, the couples scraping past, it all feels romantic somehow. And with every minute of quiet accumulating, she's afraid she got it wrong. Perhaps he wants her after all. And as this thought comes, mixed with an apprehension over what to do next, so does the clack-clack of a loud speaker and an announcement breaking through the park. The gust of noise brings her relief, an excuse to speak.

What are they saying? she asks.

You won't believe. They said that we have to go, they will close for tonight. Fuck this is a restraint. There is no reason to lock people out of a park.

She feels self-conscious. A quick sinking and slow burn up from the stomach to the skin.

He can't remember which entrance they came from. She says maybe they could ask someone. He stops, hunches down towards her, hardening his face and shoulders.

You like to ask questions. You could work for my paper. You should learn Kurdish, you know, and come work for my paper.

Sure, why not? She says, offering with all the enthusiasm that can be caught, what response might fit the easiest, but he doesn't offer the hoped for softening of his expression. Only more of the burn from stomach to skin. The weak remnants of a throbbing. She pins her eyes to the saturated hot pink and orange lights falling in the folds of black lake water, but she's still there.

He leaves town tomorrow. First back to his city and then to the border. There're articles to write and when he will return can't be said, but soon.

x

Later in the night, the Man of Small Vital Facts calls, he asks in Kurdish if she needs anything. In English she responds that she doesn't understand. In Kurdish he says she should try.

In English he tells her at least she should try.

She laughs, seeing a joke with a punch line closing in.

Do you need anything?

No.

Repeat after me, yek, one, du, two, se, three. Yek, du, se, one two three.

He laughs. *Good-bye, dear.*

Even later, smacked awake thinking she should have made a joke. Jokes can help most always, even bad ones, usually, like if she said, I could really use some Mexican food! Mexican food, a pyramid of cupcakes, any of many absent foods. Food.

x

This sort of late hour lives where jokes don't come, she finds it not so different from an hour in America. Eyes flicked open, something buzzing behind the ear—a mosquito, maybe, ghosts, black beans and cheddar cheese, another call to prayer, a hope she thought she killed off elsewhere, some quote, Wittgenstein: *You get tragedy where the tree, instead of bending, breaks.* Her eyes adjust to the dark shade of the hour. A shade she recognizes. It collects under her eyes. She imagines it will spread, crack and bulge—her face a façade, warping with time and temperature. Her body, instead of bending will break. A darkness spreading, bulging, collapsing in on her small jokeless bones.

WITH EVERY EROSION COMES DECOMPOSITION

Darkness. In the prematurely creviced face of the 12-year-old mechanic and all over the colorful murals on the downtown bomb blast walls—paintings of Saddam behind bars, or noosed, paintings of gassed bodies bloating up in piles. The sky bruised when dust storms cross the foothills, punching their way through town, pulling the whole city under. Not a throat, pore, eye or loaf of bread is spared.

MUDHAFARIA MINARET, IN 1000 WORDS OR LESS

Dropping one ancient, fragile brick at a time.

The story she would rather write, just down the road, the crouching men and sidewalk games, those small, smudgy girls clicking by in dingy nightgowns.

Wouldn't that be the story? These things not yet broken or buried. What changes and moves with the earth?

AZ, pointing past everything, says one of his brother's lives in those new high rises lining the Salahadin highway—those toy colored buildings popping from the plain on these rare, clear days. Every evening AZ's brother's wife demands her husband drive her around.

So they drive. They drive all over town. No purpose, she never wants to stop, only wants to ride around. Sometimes they will ride for over an hour, no talking. That's a chain to my brother's ankle is what you would say in America right?

Pretty much, she says listlessly.

What does she think about just riding with no destination? What does she see worth seeing again and again every night?

His wide eyes say he's waiting on her answers. She thinks of a joke to make, she wants to plant some sturdy grip. Still, so far, nothing.

WHAT ALREADY HAPPENED

8000 boys and men sharing a single name and distinguished only by the shape of the marks that lined their eyes vanished from their village one night. In place of them went rumors of their whereabouts. Clues began to flow north from the southern deserts, of Nugra Salman, where poison drifted in water, and shuttle buses led to hot iron grills and pits of angry, starving dogs.

Strangers came and cut up the land. The deserts were sliced apart, mountains cut down the middle, rivers cleaved, the people chopped into quarters, their words stabbed to death.

One Wednesday, a sweet apple smell erupted in the air, and everything began to fall—birds on cables, sheep, donkeys, tomatoes, and finally the villagers—with pain around their eyes, vomiting, confusion, tremors, the onset of blackness slanting in and over the powdery rain of chemicals. An army came from the south, and burned away the trees. Helicopters poured down gasoline, and the insides of shrines became rape havens. Some ran for the mountains, some shit in rivers, some held their children over the edge of mules to pee.

For some time there was just trench warfare, machine gun posts, bayonet charging, barbed wire, human waves, Mig 23 jets, F4 Phantoms, mechanized mountain infantry divisions, a border garrison at Qasr-e Shirin, a bullet hole through a headscarf and a molar. There were only objects.

AZ was four years old, small in this world and only able to see the smaller of objects, like broken Zippos and shoes. Especially shoes—shoes worn down and snagged on rocks, lost shoes, found shoes, shoes frozen, shoes slipping, shoes charred black with the soles peeling, shoes in trenches and under wire, shoes heard over borders, shoes rolling under mountains, shoes soaked bitter with urine and river water, shoes delicately moving, shoes and hot milk in the home of a stranger. AZ cut his ankle on a mountain, trying to keep pace with his father. The father hung his daughter over his shoulder, upside down and limp as a rice bag, as a fast fever ran through her. Close in the distance, where the mountain became Iran, long sheets of bread rose with the sunlight. Others had already arrived. They cleaned the rocky dirt from their cuts, ready to tell the arriving family that—for now at least—their cuts could scab over.

That year the national soccer team lost the game and got locked up in a cold, dark box underground to think about what went wrong. (Some versions of this story include a lion.)

Max was a water engineer, dug holes, ran pipes from the Zab River to here. Max was things that added up.

Now she passes and he says *dawstasadt. Do you know what that means? From hand to hand, one person to another. Like what I will give you when I say this: If you put the spider's skin on a wound, it will stop the bleeding. Put snake's blood around the eyes, your sight gets stronger.*

She asks, Do you need anything?

He takes a fork from his cooking apron, turns a gray coal on his stove of wires, he points.

No, God is already here for the moment.

(And still, no joke to put here.)

A German guesthouse and beer garden opens. Y says the Ethiopian prostitutes live here, imagines they could stay at worse places. Grass grows, for one, and the marigold shaped mist machines jerking at their mechanical stems keep it covered in dew, an oompah style happy birthday tune streams from a speaker rigged to a palm tree. It's not Germany, and breaded chicken patties aren't schnitzel, but the beer is real, and the beer will do.

WHAT ELSE NOW

According to the Lebanese, where he's from, a stomach as large as his means sexy.

For sure, it means you eat well and if you eat well it means you have money.

And if you have money it means you are sexy? She asks.

For sure!

And the Aussie found a duff—a whirling dervish tambourine. Beats it along to the sink of dishes, the toilet flushing, the Lebanese's foot to the rug.

And things shrink and repeat in pattern in this other life to exhaust.

And Y doesn't leave her room, she sends out only her laugh—from under the door, it flutter kicks across the house, along with the voice of a man, an accent, British maybe. It's unusual, they think and say, not like Y at all, to hide in her room with a man, to let her laugh get so far. When she finally comes through the door, smoothing her hair, no questions are asked—questions being pointless, since it isn't really clear if this is her. Since, at any given moment, this isn't any of them.

(And she finds if she spends too much time in this house, Y becomes easy to hate, especially lately—her constant smell of Burberry, skin cream, how clean she stays.)

That, and other things kept hidden. For example, beyond the fence line, the nightly bullion of far off trash fires send light toward the rooftop—leaves her longing to have seen the ignition occur, and the stray black flakes of charred paper.

And the moon. A flick of bug in light and the moon, this cross section. They all agree the moon's bigger here, bigger than elsewhere. No one knows why. And what O wouldn't give to get stoned right now.

Tonight the Lebanese will fall asleep in a chair. O will have an egg at his ear, ready to smash—

Oh, I will do it. I will fucking do it!

(Also: Some stories still in progress and yet to be revealed, like O and the cigarette she's snuck with the University's gardener and how this will, in a few days, lead to a trip behind the gym trailer and dumpsters, where he keeps a tuna-fed monkey from Iran.)

BAYANE BASH: GOOD MORNING

The driver starts the car.

I hate this.

I'm sorry.

Don't apologize.

Slowly turning the key in the ignition.

AZ, from the backseat, says he suffers from *the universal condition of boredom.*

The editor-in-chief's nephew, just back from a tour of
Swedish Universities, lanky legs and fingers, bright new
Pumas, spinning office chairs, the manic flipping of cable
stations. He may go to Sweden, he says, but he'd rather study
in America.

Though that's much harder—harder with no wife.

He could marry her, he says, and get to America that way.

She juggles his words. Balled-up jokes, tossed up, clutched
and tossed.

She says, I'd have to get a paycheck first, before we could go
anywhere.

The room laughs—

(Finally. Flattery.)

WHAT CHRONIC PATTERNS EMERGE

Dreams. She moves around them, her room and B, synching
up, Sam Cook mp3s, a cheek on a cheek, as though, yes, this
is what should be, stopping at the mirror to watch the frame
from neck bone to pelvis. This mirror where she appears,
nights before bed and again the morning after, more ugly,
puffy eyed, dim, dark wishes, stares, secret little stare-downs.

The Man of Small Vital Facts. His visits heaping. Before
they reach the bar they drive, never going far, but staying
within the circular roads that ring out from the city center.
With these drives comes the ease of routine, the decline
of his aimless chatter, a stilling of the surface. Even an
otherwise sharp turn left or right gets soft with a melancholy
stride. What noise emerges, his voice or hers, comes sporadic
in the form of predictable questions. *Hungry?* He asks and
no she never is. *Cold with the windows down?* No she never is.
Even the music hiccups—1 of 3 rotating Kurdish CDs,
simple melodies of synthesizer and violin.

Love songs we call heyrans, he says, *with lyrics too sad to explain.*

(These nights end with O on the couch.

Watch yourself. I think you daydream about him.

I guess it's safer at the Edge?

Only take what you need, love.)

Daydreams. Him, maybe, not so much in form, but a delicate force. Some gust tickling her toward something familiar, taking over where another left off, taking over with the other still there. A reminder she's still intact. Like now— at the stove, tapping a spoon, waiting for water to boil, one of B's Nietzsche quotes from the steam, said while chewing fried oysters, grinning, January, a baby blue leather diner booth. *Why does man not see things? He is himself standing in the way, he conceals things.* And then water over the lip of the pot, the burn yanking her back. The darkness. She feels around for the hole of light to breath through—

WHAT ACCUMULATES

Late fall at the villa. O's switched out cigarettes with a
nargilla. The room slurps with pipe water, reeking red
flavored tobacco, strawberry, cherry, bubble gum. The Aussie
switched out the duff with anecdotes—one about being
drunk and smuggling pumpkins across the Canadian border,
one about having his thumb sucked by a calf in a dark field.

These moments begin with O rising from the couch to pack
another nargilla pipe, as the Aussie begins to tell a story,
then the Lebanese shifts his gut on the couch, each time less
contained in his white tank top.

And Y, now back, her room no longer leaking a British
accent. And she's quieter. Tonight, in the kitchen, her spine
tight, the rim of a teacup to her chin, thinking, maybe, of all
the places she isn't and all the people that aren't.

Paper balls on the office floor. AZ's transcripts, letters of
recommendation, resume, exam results—4 points shy of a
Fulbright.

He says, *Why bother?*

Kurdish plots for escape. Claim political asylum in Malaysia.
Lose a passport in New Zealand. Bus it to Turkey. Boat it to
Lebanon/Greece. Pass the TOEFLE. Get the Fulbright.

Misfires. The editor-in-chief wants a column about adjusting
to Kurdistan. A thousand words a week of all the ways she

loves it here. His voice cracks from the speakerphone.

You could call it Making Friends in the Mountains.

I was thinking an article about the homeless, she says.

Funny. There are no homeless here, my friend.

I know someone.

Even funnier. We must discuss the difference between tribal and homeless.

No, I know—

I've got another call hold on.

Following a discussion about Angelina Jolie and Brad Pitt: AZ slapping his laptop, nearly knocking the ashtray, rising from the couch.

Do you know how to tell if a bride from this country loves her husband?

No.

Leaning in, hushed: *You must look through the wedding pictures and see how happy she looks. If she looks too happy she isn't. If she looks sad she probably isn't.*

I don't get it. And why this now?

Hushing more for emphasis: *She is being ridiculed for her love. If she really loves him they will know it and it is the wrong sort of marriage.*

But if she's smiling it could mean she really loves him, right?

Well, yes, but only if her eyes look freer than she does.

Of course!

What do you mean of course?

Nothing!

Back to where she was: the print ad for Baghdad's gold district warming her desk, some scrambled photo of a sunset framed by the black silhouette of cascading palm leaves, a cluster of gold bracelets, rings hung in a white-lit storefront.

(Better this photo, than this room.)

On the Swedish channel, a Smiths song—"How Soon is Now?"—and some dull, old faithful ache attached. The electricity cuts, midway with the song, in the dense hour of final edits. The office clunks with frustration. She feels out the remainder of the song in a hum, soft, unnoticed.

(She wonders: what can be done when it's no longer audible, but still speaking in you?)

Seatbelts. Seemingly irrelevant here. She finds she doesn't use them. No one does, and rarely does it occur to her, regardless of how rough the road and turns, regardless of the just-dodged semis and goats. Especially late Tuesdays, or well into Wednesday morning, heading home after the week's issue goes to press, the truck beyond capacity, shaking through the sleeping villages. These nights, it seems impossible that something could break the moment, as though suddenly nothing's subject to mortal grounds. She inserts herself, part of the indestructible structure. These arms and legs, the folk songs loud in the ears, the musk of another's sweat, slurred coughs, the red-eyed who explain what the folk song really means, the friction of another's exhausted knee bone, an inability to move no matter what— these brief, speeding rides move her forward.

CHAWA-KANIM LEK-NA: I CLOSED MY EYES

Now come the moped and the roped dog. A moped a rope and a dog just as stringy.

RWASTA: STOP

Here. One of those nights, in a queue of nights that haven't beginnings or ends. A night tightening in and insects fill her head. He glances at her quickly then pulls the car over suddenly, near the dank stretch of fence line, where men come to drink out of sight. For a moment, quiet and darkness, his fume smell, a clicking of the car's warm engine settling.

Okay. Let's do something different, he whispers enthusiastically. *I've got something.*

He looks straight ahead now, as though still driving in his mind. She wonders if this is how it happens. Her first kiss in a foreign country, first sign that someone here, beyond the random feral-eyed strangers passed on the street or sitting in the bar, wants to fondle her hair, her breasts or clutch for the throbbing burrowed between her legs. A peak of light says: Let the hope not be killed. Let what comes come fast and sudden, unhampered by thought.

He turns and angles toward the backseat, pulls a laptop up from the floor. Opening it, he balances it over the gearshift.

My pictures from America, he says, his smile proud, too much teeth.

Of course! She says. That sudden fit of small ticks.

x

He says some pictures were taken in towns with names
bogged down by too many syllables, names he can't
remember. He flashes through shots full of tall gray statues,
bridges, harbors of green water with something called *jellyfish*
blinking on the surface. There were nightclubs. He says the
nightclubs had mirrored balls, big lights that hurt to look
at and music spilling out to the sidewalk. In the nightclubs,
everything moved the way things move in dreams. He'd
danced with an American girl, who wore her hair in bright
red braids, and later in a nearby diner they'd taken pictures.

Most of the pictures include him and his fellow exchange
students, flashing peace signs, cocked heads and gaping
smiles, poised next to fountains and buildings. But the
pictures of him and the girl show something different—a
late night diner, a girl snaking her red braids over his
shoulder, tugging his *I Love New York* t-shirt, tipping on their
stools, her puckered mouth firm to his cheek.

A snicker rises from her throat. Ha! Looks like you got
along pretty well there.

The words arrive reckless, missing her usual placidity.
Instead, an ache comes. An urge to toss the laptop into the
windshield.

If you could go again, would you? She asks, saying the
first thing that comes. The question delivered with no real

thought, just a sudden pressure to say something that might bury the last several minutes.

Again his quiet. The rare pause. He flips down the laptop— the moment gone with the machine's blue light.

He's somewhere in the distance now, but exactly where she doesn't know. Only quiet darkness surrounds. Darkness in the flickering gnats, in the silhouettes of men peeing at the fence line, between shards of whiskey bottles in the dirt. The darkness smears down her face and she waits.

SOMETIMES THREE CLICKS OF THE TONGUE IS GOOD. OTHER TIMES, IT'S BAD.

With breath comes answers to questions, but this morning's answer comes back wrong.

This is not the world! How could you think that? Look around you!

The driver dramatically lifts his hand, points toward
the long, gray road ahead and the gritty haze veiling the
foothills. Nothing moves, but a flitting dot of buzzards.

You need to understand your reasons for being here.

(And the roads grow in rings, and apathy keeps going into
answers, and there seems to be new construction each day
and most everything remains unhinged: along sidewalks,
stones poke sharp, in the dome of dinging wood, rope
against metal makes the wind siren, endless wires, layers of
cement, whittled down tree trunks, debris, debris, debris,
baby chicks stirring dirt, stray road cattle and the figures
in the field, facing Mecca, long and bending for prayer on
beautiful blue mats. With breath or no breath, answers or no
answers, everything plummets around her, thinning toward
the bone, both hard and hardly.)

II

BUN-AWA:
TO BREAK INTO PIECES

A small fact: when the car's full of too many religions, races and genders—you avoid Kirkuk altogether, sticking to unpredictable, steep, thin roads around Lake Dukon. Such as now, the Man of Small Vital Facts, taking her to Suleimania for New Year's Eve, along with two others—his journalist friends—a Chaldean Christian woman and Sunni Muslim man. As they drive, he turns on ABBA and she hides how funny she finds it. A Tuborg beer between his thighs, tapping a cigarette on the dash to Mama Mia. This, she concludes, is him happy.

Blackness out there, where the lake would be, no light but the pierce comma moon. She turns into herself, yellow with beer on an empty stomach, tries to determine if she cares it's a holiday. From the backseat a loud conversation begins between the Chaldean and Sunni, and she understands little, chooses to process even less. As a small object dangling from a weak thread, right now she could fall loose and leave them too large to see where she landed.

Hey!

A voice comes in English, poking from the back seat.

The Man of Small Vital Facts pushes his eyes over the wire of his glasses.

Sorry for our behavior.

x

As they approach the city limits, she mishears the question he asks.

She answers, No!...Oh yes! I'm great. Just tired. Long day.

What he's asked is, when they get to Suleimania's checkpoint, would she drive the car through? Just through the checkpoint. He has no license. Never has, on principle of course, and he's sorry he didn't mention it sooner, but since it's a holiday they may actually check the cars tonight. So, it's safer that way, with her driving.

Sorry. It will be fine.

The checkpoint reminds her of a highway tollbooth. Later she tells him this, laughing, and assures him that yes, it was in fact fine. Then he laughs, the two laughs slapping together. It fills the car, beckons her out of herself. She returns to her place in the car.

Once inside the city they hit the idle gridlock of everyone everywhere, not quite where they'd hoped by midnight. The Chaldean and Sunni hold hands. Words thin out to saccharine mumbles. She thinks, this town could be

anywhere—a road strewn with pastel paper, the thump of
stressed car stereos, Rihanna's song "Umbrella," glitter on a
passing hat. She tries to determine if this makes her happy.

x

Arriving at an empty two story cinderblock house, two
men sit on the doorstep, one in flip flops, neither in a coat,
screaming angry English—angry since they've flown in from
Baghdad, have waited all night in the cold for this car to pull
up. Not even the women are home tonight and everyone's
come hungry.

x

Until the man in flip-flops left the room, until she confused
his cries for laughs, things had clicked along easy. The
stinking heat of the propane stove, splitting fava beans from
their shiny dry skins, the Chaldean falls asleep with her
head on the lap of the Sunni, *Men in Black II* on TV, the ice
disappearing but the whisky not. By the time he reenters the
room, they've translated his crying for her and the story of
his fiancé and the car bomb.

Not for a thousand angels. I would give a thousand angels to bring her.

(Another of his small, vital facts: *If you are from where I am from, if you drink with us, someone in the room will always begin to cry and the night will not end until this happens. That is when you know it is time to stop.*)

Sea glass green a blue-violet static then blank.

She wakes in another year's cool, weak light, swelling up the paisleys in the curtains. On the floor, everyone sleeps, curled toward the long-cold propane stove. The house now shuffles and creaks with people. The door opens and shuts quick, a girl peeks in—his sister, a cousin, a brother's wife, maybe. Sounds, lights, objects, all gets filtered through the residuals of whisky. She fakes sleep. Nestled in those not knowing moments, she stays comfortable there while it lasts.

Breakfast. The girl who may or may not have peeked through the door, who's eventually known as his sister—F—lugs away the propane stove and sleeping mats, spreads out a plastic sheet covered in cherries and humming birds—fried eggs, naan, yogurt, tea pot, glasses, honey. F moves fast, speaks with taunt nods and eyebrow lifts. She has his sea glass eyes, his hardness.

This morning includes no English, and what she doesn't know grows. Ideas, answers, debates, where the other guests will go next. Under the noise of what's undecipherable, the words she can translate bob up buoyant, changing her dull smirk to a smile. The other guests brush her with occasional gazes.

(He'll tell her later just how they took her soft eyes and quiet, shifting mouth as signs of an agreeable nature. *Timid maybe. Odd for an American*, they'd all said.

I thought it was best to tell them they were right.

He smiles and she rolls her eyes like a teenager.)

Agreeable, maybe, but more so passive with stiffness, tired, and sore-boned from a night on the floor. Agreeable, maybe, since she gives little and asks for even less, accepts decisions made, like, how she'll stay here ten more days. He'd rather not take her back any sooner and he'd like her to stay for a party next week, and with her paper on hiatus, she doesn't argue, finds relief in relinquishing control over when to be where.

Suleimania, midday, no signs of a holiday now and she decides she likes it that way, finds it somehow freeing, dashing past electronics and the labyrinth of clothing merchants, F's fingers locked gentle and urgent at her knuckles. Occasionally F squeezes the hand—it says, stay close.

Sweet pistachio steam fills the air, flies milk the thick goat cheese. She holds the hand tight. She will stay close today. She will stay intact.

At a clothing stall in the bazaar F insists her new friend try on the traditional folk dress—loud, rose pink sequins, loose as a drape. F ties the long sleeve ends behind her waist for her.

Cocooned, hardly room to raise, a maze of gossamer folds to maneuver. F laughs.

Yes, this is the problem.

Clothes should not be problems, she scoffs.

And but I wear them every day!

WHAT'S NOT PREPARED FOR

Washing at the home of another: Let hosts do as they insist,
boiling stove pots of water, enough for two bowls—one to
soap and one to rinse. (Never let this seem inconvenient/
more than what's needed/less than what's desired.)

Light. Collect the last, to keep the room from pressing
shut as long as possible. Delay the loss of hands in the lap,
the faces of others, the eating away of walls, the clock, the
old, red rug. Spread the curtains wide. Soon, but not soon
enough, something will click—something will come through
the sockets. Something will send volts through the wires.
For the first few seconds, just a putter noise, then tick and
the room comes blue and twitching with kerosene flames,
the smooth sound of water pressure, steam in the cool, steel
bowl, all the music, vibration, television, *Prison Break, Seinfeld,
Friends.*

Some things not translatable:
Is she Christian?
Yes, of course.
His quick turn and whisper, *Just say yes you are Christian. It is
the only option.*

The impossible to translate.

In this environment, his sea glass eyes—more glass and less
sea—an avalanche could grow out of the smallest falling dot
of a rock.

Everything going under quickly.

WHAT'S ON TOP

Even when cold or dark, the house carousels. Children, tangles of hair, snot paste, a kitchen of women, deliberate, sunny gestures, fried eggs, a steady rotation of slow moving men. She marvels inward at the emphasis placed on what she'd always considered throw-away tasks: the way the water boils for dish washing, the way the dish washing makes way for the cutting of cucumbers.

Everyone's friendly, curious about the American and her quiet, agreeable nature. They ask about her American life, and she answers with breezy anecdotes—family, pets, friends, school, work, food. She keeps it centered at the dull and obvious, as though chatting with a grandparent. They would never understand beyond that, she assumes. To tell them everything might mean to lose them altogether and right now she has just enough.

Everyone. She likes them, but most of all E—the niece, the crouched corner girl, stitching sequins to a blue lace scarf, sewing needles slipping from her perfect little lips. At 14, she's grown too fast into sensual features and has no idea. Her dreams flop out in broken English. Today it's Australia. Why Australia E couldn't say, at least not in English, but she's sure to go. If she doesn't, if she stays here, she wants to kill all the boys in this town. Some day she wants to be president, line them all at the wall, shoot them one by one.

You wouldn't believe it but we once had a library. We once had books. . .
and beds, more furniture. Fuck this.

Slamming the cabinet, table legs screeched on cement,
rubbing his temple veins hard and gray. Her empathy,
mechanical, she says, it's okay, don't worry about it.
But he really wants to find her this book—this book he
demands she'll want. And in some ways she wants it found,
taking to the idea of an object travelling from him to her.
But still, no, it's fine, stop looking. Anything but him angry,
anything but the ignition that comes from small frustrations,
the rockets of furniture, burn-hole pillows, smoldering
hours.

Daylight moves through this house. His clear outline cuts with no warning.

In 1990, he turned 10, Iraq accused Kuwait of stealing oil,
the family plotted their route from Baghdad. First, they sold
their balcony birdcage, filled with hundreds of tiny yellow
and red lovebirds. When the sun would rise, the birds would,
too. Their bright chirps steady until the house settled, after
the men left and the women had finished scraping honey
from the plates.

Soon after went the fig tree, the beds, the couch, the
bookshelves and books.

What they took: The framed portrait of their father, a pink
plastic bowl, a cupboard of matchsticks, flour, honey, 7
wool-woven blankets and a cotton bag.

(The framed portrait of their father. A man on a roof, a
kalishnakoff rifle slung over a shoulder, a white and red scarf
on a head, hard creviced mouth, sea glass eyes.
On the other side of the wall that holds the portrait, his
sister's warming a plate of walnuts near black on the propane
stove and their mother eats them for her sick, bad, heart.
She should be resting but instead, she's stirring onions
in sunflower oil, chewing walnuts, forcing more naan on
the American, speaking at her in Kurdish, enthusiastically,
pointing a wooden spoon at the window. The American
registers six of her words: *you, I, girl, go, young, jail.* She nods,
smiles, flushed—not the audience this woman deserves.)

West of Suleimania, where serrated black rocks of the
Zagros range cut Iraq from Iran, she meets his eldest brother
and brother's children.

Imagine right there.

The brother only speaks in English, laughing against the
wind, his meaty fingers cupping her shoulders, her muscles
startled stiff beneath the abrupt grip. He shifts her toward
a break in spiny rock, where the road meets the valley. A
swatch of green, an endless globe of nickel.

*There. Imagine a B-52 now out of nowhere and going downdown
downdown push me down in there, go ahead and push me down and I
will fall but I will live!*

His sons laughing, his daughters squeal no.

(He becomes known as the Man Who Punched Out Horses
in the War, having done just that.)

Things not given or sold, just lost include the family mule, his mother's best white scarf, some baby chicks, almonds, raisons and garlic, the tweezers, the elegant arch of their eyebrows, the kneading of their dough.

WHEN YOU FIND THEM DIG THEM UP AND LET THEM REST

On the television, the woman in black hijab holds a framed picture with one hand and places the other lightly to each coffin, right as they go one by one, row by row, sunk in the earth.

E explains why.

They put people in the ground with no food or water and then they died. They buried babies and they were alive. Now they find them and put them where they go.

Tonight, for his newspaper's annual party, he'd rather she wear his sister's traditional dress, but here she can go no further, so they compromise at F's acrylic explosion of turquoise and tan flowers, tight at the torso, loosening at the knees, a cream jacket, tan nylons, brown boots, golden eyeliner, electric pink rouge, mud colored lipstick, hair ironed flat, settled and flowing in one precise direction.

Her experiment, F calls this shut-eyed girl, as she clamps the hair straightener at her scalp, the roots tugged sore in the grip, the iron moving past the dead end tips. F pulls lightly at her experiment's chin, says, *if you don't have your ears pierced next time you visit I will kill you. It's that simple.*

(*Simple.* The word, here, has nowhere to go. And she wants to smudge it all off, the sudden build-up, the broken reflection in the mirror.)

They take her picture, instruct her to smile. Beyond her thick pasty face, beyond the picture's frame, the family moves from room to room, task to task—their lives actual, dense with context and in no need of explanation. The mother, softly curled on a thin sleeping mat, eats warm walnuts for her heart.

(Here she arrives where she can go no further.)

x

At the party, he leads the dance—sets the motion that links the arms and keeps the chain turning. The music bangs

and jolty riffs vibrate, the women yank in cool silver ear
hoops, loose bright cords over hips, the winter wind hits
the window and his movements, his muscles, his breathy
joints—a slight bend of the wrist, graceful knee bend
that keeps the circle steered, centered. When not dancing,
he's bumming cigarettes, grabbing shoulders, laughing at
everything, breathing so easily.

Somewhere else but near, on a white plastic chair at a long
table of children and cake crumbs, she takes one napkin and
one Parliament cigarette from his pack for every song he
leads.

WHAT ELSE GETS QUESTIONED

The women of the house, the ones not yet sleeping—the ones who can recall English when sleepy—want her to explain what's going on. *Friends*: the bold white Arabic scroll on the screen crosses out Ross's neck. He argues with Phoebe, they drink coffee. Things are falling from focus, the dark air takes the sharpness. She's a tired, conscientious spine pressed against a sleeping mat, tucked under a silver cavern of cigarette smoke. She explains, concealing how much effort it takes to do so, that Phoebe loves a man who leaves for Minsk. He comes back in another season, but they find it's too late to realize their love. The electricity cuts for the night.

Where's Minsk? They ask her, unfazed by the black out.

(Other questions include, or will include: *Do you really want to be a journalist? Do you really have passion? Here? Why do you not marry?*)

She begins to say she just doesn't know and her words fizzle to sighs. The sighs, diluted in the sharp, dark air, disappear. Then just the air comes. Someone snores beside her. She has no outline against it now—loses the wavering oval cup of her hands, the rise and fall of the foot as it finds a new position, the hook of the arm at the hip. The room begins to sleep.

E wants to give her the scarf she's sewn, pleads with her to take it. When she doesn't, E asks, *Why?* E waits until she leaves the room, shoves it in her purse, attaches a pencil-sketched kangaroo.

Why? Too shapeless a question to bother with anymore. Easily thrown far out of range.

Driving towards the café he proudly claims will remind her of America, he answers a call—a sigh, a pause, some urgent whispers, then hands her the phone.

Hello?

In her ear tumbles female sobs, and undecipherable Kurdish. She hands the phone back and he ends the call, looks her way, says *thank you.*

What did she say? She asks.

Even if you bothered to learn Kurdish, I've said already some things are just impossible to translate.

Why'd you hand me the phone?

Cha wit pe haldene.

She what?

Jealous. *Ato Salmandneky Zindwy.*

A ghostly thin voice—a sentence drifts and she lets it go. He pries her hand from her lap, squeezing the index and middle fingers, releasing. Letting them land where they will. The hand stays where it lands rigid and cool.

You know, if your Kurdish improved, you could come work for my paper.

And do something important?

Yes.

I've got a few excuses as to why that might be difficult.

I've got excuses for not accepting that.

(She wants to punch his face, but no. And at the café, only
the napkins remind her of America. She takes as many
as possible. A stash for the toilet, her secret, snagging in
her pocket's crease as she walks, so grateful for this secret.
Tonight she has this secret.)

What they have acquired includes a kitchen table and three chairs, most anything for cooking, a wall to hang the father's portrait, a car.

Day ten. Tonight he'll take her home, but first to Kirkuk to drop off the brother who punched horses in the war. In the winter-damp backseat, she stares at her knees, avoids what rushes past—rather the collision before the knowing. Still, she can tell the size and nearness of vehicles by the girth of rattles. She tallies the rattles, compares the size of one with the last.

The brother points out where a B52 once dropped a bomb. A crater in the foothill. She sees only sad rolling plains of tan.

He says that, along with punching horses, they would also punch each other. *Straight in the face, right in the trenches, no gas mask.*

Kirkuk. Cement bags and window bars. Oil fields tinge the sky gold with fire. Looks like no morning could lift away this night. He jumps from the car quick, white shirt loose in the wind, coat forgotten. As he shrinks in the rear window, she fingers the zipper of his coat, already wishing she'd said to stop the car, already wishing she'd been bold enough to ask: What happens to a punched out horse?

(Beyond Kirkuk limits, a restaurant at a highway rest stop, eating kabob he says, *Don't speak loud, sit next to me here.*)

I'll say this. There's moments we forget ourselves and that's when we can be ourselves, don't you agree? It's terrible we should have to regret that. Anything we do in those moments we are ourselves. What I'm saying is, it's hard not being our self. Like living in a cage.

She laughs, tells him Nietzsche says people are like shop windows. We rearrange ourselves, either hiding or showing off the traits that other people ascribe to us.

I used to think being in a cage was most a problem just in this part of the world. But maybe it's everywhere's problem. Did you say shop windows? I don't understand this.

Nothing.

Can I tell you about something?

Sure?

I loved a married woman, she wasn't just married, she was married to a friend. I mean a colleague, a journalist, back in Suleimania. I took her as mine, because she said that if I didn't, she'd be with everyone and I felt I had to be with her to protect her from herself, to keep her from being with everyone. Now she's threatening to tell her husband if I don't sleep with her again soon.

Wow.

I'm actually a little frightened.

That's fucked. So, how does this relate to feeling like yourself?

That isn't the point. I thought maybe you would understand.

I do.

Maybe not.

Stop.

Not so loud, not here.

Sorry.

There's this thing that happens with girls in my country—

I know.

Tell me something? Something interesting to feel better.

So I guess you feel pretty trapped.

Never mind. Please something. Tell me.

Okay…I think I've forgotten how to be funny?

Stop. Tell me.

What that's not good enough? Well…let's see, I—

You never speak of love. Why? Tell me something of who you have loved.

What I love? It's not relevant. What I love isn't relevant.

You mean who *not* what.

No difference.

But are you being yourself? To love this dead?

I don't have an answer to that.

If you were yourself you would know. You should have an answer, you choose this not being yourself.

And I'd be funny.

You are funny, of course, you are American. And being American means you have luxury to not be yourself, right?

Oh yeah. Right. Of course. Fuck you. We all have that right and not all Americans are funny.

No need to be angry. I only want to know about him. Please. It will help me feel better. Don't you care for that?

It's like this. The dead thing, it used to recite philosophy to me, when we'd fight. The kind of philosophy you get into in high school. Existentialism, stuff like Nieztche, you know?

Any time I did something this dead thing didn't like it would recite philosophy. Like it was teaching me a lesson. I hated it. Really it was the only thing I hated about this thing, when he'd become a patronizing fuck. So I have to think about these moments, these quotes and remember how annoyed I would get. Actually, it's gotten sort of compulsive. Like, I'll see how many things in one hour I can relate to a stupid Nietzsche quote. And then I start to think the more quotes, the closer I'm getting to being over this dead thing. It's ridiculous.

I know that word...Philosophy. But I can't remember what it means.

It's what people talk about when they don't want to talk about the real problem.

I don't get this thing you say about shopping windows.

I'm full.

The restaurant: Roughly a year from now, she'll think it's the one on CNN. Crushed like a stomped can, glass and gravel, the parking lot, a charred crescent, scooped out blackness. She'll want to tell Everyone but tells No One instead.

III

HESHTIN:
TO LET GO

Back in Erbil, roommates Y and O just returning from their holiday in Jordan have an *oh-shit-I'm-back* sensation. It hit when the plane landed on all that bland dust and rock. After two weeks gone, something between a joke and a plot's begun. Because sometimes you got to make it into something else. Something funny—all this *Christ I'd rather be dead than more this*. So, you lift it up and look from the other end, notice how much it resembles something else. Call it anything, anything else. Like jokes about suicide. Take the spiral staircase, they say, and take a rope, take the bucket and the cart from the half finished house next door, take anything sharp, take a cinder block, take a few of Y's scarves knotted tight, take a fist. What a spectacle, what a catastrophe, what a way to make light float, with all those hard tile steps swooping up through the middle of this ridiculous villa.

O's laughing at her own jokes, spills the cherry tobacco everywhere. It coats the kitchen sticky, pulpy, loud pink tobacco, and it couldn't be better timed, this spill, a gory bloom ignored. It says *just let go for now*.

(But Erbil feels good somehow and she's just glad not to
sleep on the floor tonight. Glad to be funny and understood
no matter how fast the words get said. Glad that today
brings everything quick and bright, a perfect balance
between light and object, plot and joke, past and now, the
hard grooved roads, the weak kneed donkey, mud caked
joints, cracking, carting the town's ice blocks, the sunflowers
puckered with dust in hung man droops, the stink of
propane in her coat, the stink of his house, each time she
pulls it over her shoulders, his mother's warm walnuts, two
long silver braids over a hot plate, sifted sunflower seeds
between fingers.)

The young Kurdish woman in the yard missed her, doesn't understand why she left town at all, made her promise she'd stay through the night. But now, far past breakfast, the woman kneels and scrubs the kitchen floor, refuses help, shoos the American back to the corner of cushions, says no sit, sit, stay. An out is needed away from all this sitting, tea, pomegranate seeds. She decides what she knew all along: this sitting helps nothing.

From the bathroom she calls O, pleads for her to be sick and in need, says, Come on. Please. Just call me and say you need something.

I could use some tobacco, actually.

Well, there you go!

Have you learned yourself a lesson, dear?

Shut up.

—his idling car at her villa gate, the guards no longer
fazed, his questions as to where she's been, why her phone's
gone unanswered. Why. She can explain, she assures with
a tired softness in her throat, climbing in, then another
complication: the young Kurdish woman in her yard, a
slant figure bouncing in the side view mirror, watching her
American friend ride away with a man.

It speeds her heart—races a hollow sound to her head and
her darkness. Through the window, neck craned up, she yells
back at it all: I've done nothing!

(At dinner, down two tables, a honey haired girl in a pink silk gown dressed like a fairy tale. The way she crinkles the sleeves and picks at her lipstick says she's too young to have dressed this way much, says she's too young to be here—14 at best—in this hotel lounge. Maybe this is her mother with all the gold and black lip liner. Maybe these are her sisters in the sheer headscarves and tight blue jeans.

Yes, because they work here. They work here for the men. Don't watch.

A small vital fact she could do without.)

Drunk. He comes in the house for once. First the bathroom, then to smoke and now this game—lights off, faces nearly touching, a lighter lit between and eye-level.

He says *look into my eye until it looks like an eye no more.*

No I can't.

Yes, don't laugh, stay still.

But she laughs, looks away, looks again and focuses.

What does it look like?

I don't know.

Figure it out.

I don't know, but it doesn't look like an eye anymore.

(This, until the game wanes, and his snores like drill bits to boulders in the floor.)

Morning. Some places it's normal, but not here now.
Sunlight and embarrassment, prisms in juice glasses, his eyes
saying it's not right—sitting at a breakfast table with three
western women.

It's getting late and he's got interviews, threatens to shower at
the bazaar's bathhouse. She won't have it, not with this—her
shower the size of a child's nursery.

And that is the problem precisely! He whispers urgent and nervous.

There! Your shopping windows! She yells. But he's gone
already so nothing gets heard and she could drop all these
dishes and spend the whole day smoothing the broken
shards into the floor with her cheeks.

WHAT GETS SO DARK, IT'S NOT SO DARK AT ALL

O walking the street with a tumbler of iced vodka coffee, news from England, something in her mother's breast, going from fruit pit to golf ball.

She asks O, Are you going to go home?

Of course not. That thing's growing no matter where I am.

True, but—

I said no, love.

Then pointing, O squeals, *Max in a box!*

And Max on the sidewalk, legs flopping out of a cardboard box—Max, the box, both dog-eared and greasy.

He says, *I'm sorry, ladies. I'm sorry.*

Above all this, a sudden star begins to stud the otherwise flat night sky. She likes to think this is more than a star—the way it veers from white to red. She likes to think the world underneath sees more than a star, more than a man in a box.

The Chaldean journalist invites her and the Man of Small
Vital Facts to a cousin's wedding and two whiskies in,
he wants to slow dance with her, though he never has, as
Muslims do it, this kind of dancing—one on one, too close
at the hips and shoulders.

As though puppetry, she aligns the arms and legs, explains
that's it, really. Simple.

And maybe it's the moment, this new public dance, the
shoulders connected and small step motions, but he's talking
softer than usual, slower, says he's got these two choices. *A
job offer here, full-time in Erbil with Voice of Iraq or back to Baghdad,
where the real work is.*

What does she think of that, he wants to know, how would
she feel to have him further or closer?

This has to do with the married girl? She asks.

I should have not involved you.

His questions wash the room into her ears. In the whoosh
she says she can't say yes, she can't say no. So he'll go back to
Baghdad, he says, if she has no opinion.

It's where I belong, maybe.

Okay, she says. No opinion. She searches for an opinion.

(Slipping down the crest of the whoosh, not knowing what else to say, because she can't tell another where to go and can't say for sure that she cares. He'd be safe anywhere, even there, never hurt, never unable to duck or run for cover, no matter.)

Then silence. The kind of silence she could use. The silence that guides toward elsewhere—not the dark crook where things fall lost, but the bright shoot where things feather down and continue. She's dancing, she realizes, and then she hears music.

She continues.

And a day follows. In it, some birds line the web of exposed beams zigzagging through the cement shell of the unfinished house next door. Some landing, some moving on.

And the young Kurdish woman stands in her yard. She doesn't talk to the American anymore, having seen her with that man, having believed her when she lied. Little more now than a smile behind hung laundry. The American smiles back, with an urge to tear each garment from the line, one by one, or just walk by in a sleeveless shirt, but no.

She continues and most days, riding to the paper, she passes the mechanic shop and the ten-year-old small man of impossible tasks, sprawled tiny under trucks propped crooked on wiggling jacks. Six times per week times six months means 144 chances to witness this child pinned to the earth.

She continues and the driver always brings his lectures. Says things like *you can't go forward in a backward place. The only time you come close to this is when you leave home and return after a long time away.*

To which she says, That reminds me of a question: Why does man not see things? Because he stands in the way. He conceals things.

The driver says, *My point to you is, you may go home soon. Some things will happen.*

Oh, you know, they better!

Bara rast-kirdinawa!

Barawhat?!

(Lately, she won't try understanding. Hardly ticks up the words she gets, can scrap it all. Goes free. The roads growing shorter, the blocks narrower. Things shrink and repeat in their dark turning patterns.)

DAWR: TO TURN CIRCLES

Where are we going?

Main Street, I told you. I told you we'd go for the dough and meat. I don't know how to say it in your language but it's dough and meat and it's like a sandwich. You aren't hungry?

I just didn't know you meant now. It's late.

And we need to discuss something. But first we eat.

She cracks the window, to knock loose the tight air inside, sucking in some landscape, the passing blacked out blocks and patches quivering white where the lights aren't yet cut. She keeps her face to the glass. The light, his cool reflection, too near.

At Main Street, she waits in the car—his request—and everything pulses with huddled men, the hack of their coughs and small trash fires. It feels somehow comforting, in this late hour, in this quiet car going cold. The way they wring their hands over fire says that here, as anywhere, cold's cold, night's night, what's home stays home, what's waiting waits.

A flash comes to her and goes—to complicate the picture by walking right in, putting her own hands over the fire, say hello.

He returns with a steaming plastic bag.

It's dough and meat.

She lays the bag in her lap. The heat needles her thigh, painful and relieving.

Why aren't you eating?

She opens the bag and tears off an awkward piece, ground meat falling lost in the seat, she hands him a piece, then another. He grabs her hand and says, *no more. Why aren't you eating?*

Not hungry. Hey, how do you think the night would go if I just walked up to that fire over there?

Dear, we need to discuss something.

I think you call this *kifta* in your language. But in my language, who knows?

Tomorrow he leaves for Baghdad, he says—*just the Green Zone, just for a while, he stresses. Come to the airport, please, to say goodbye.* His eyes now more sea, less glass.

Of course, she says. The only reply that comes.

Then the key to ignition, the choke and turning engine, the night's dust kicked from under the wheels spinning away.

The world holds so much dust.

Away. A brisk hug and his backpack loose from his shoulder, knocking her, an off balance moment. He thanks her in a rickety voice she thinks sounds out-of-character shy, but realizes quick that he's nervous. She says she will always admire him for leaving. This makes sense to say, she thinks, and assumes she probably means it—admires him for doing something at all, for going away from whatever he's leaving, past the airport friction, the madness, behind frosted terminal doors, midair, pushed toward a direction too late to stop.

In her wave and small smile, grief and a tinge of relief she won't bother making sense of.

(Space, once again, so much stretching between her and another. Space stretching and the world gets so far stretched.)

Y calls, finally, several hours after leaving for her jog—the word *fucking* jumping from her delicate mouth, out through the phone receiver. *Fucking*, over the dings and static of hospital noise and a child's wail, as she waits to have her arm bandaged.

Someone tried to yank me into a fucking jeep.

BARA RAST-KIRDINAWA: TO GET STRAIGHT A CROOKED LOAD

From the rooftop, gray sun over mountain snow
uncomfortably grows in the eye, a painful mirror. She'd never
have thought it could get so cold here or the villa so still.

She goes to a restaurant where there's soup, and a pack of
Chinese gum bought from that bazaar boy—his stuck-out
tongue, scrunched face, and arms of protest, just beyond the
restaurant glass. His tongue fractures the solace that comes
while eating soup alone in a crowd. She hasn't yet bought
enough gum, and he can wait all day—follow her through
the bazaar, kiss her elbow, call her *mister, mister, please, mister.*
Leaving the restaurant, she buys more, but still not enough.
He follows, to the taxi, the shut door, the rolled up window.
Something in her says go and fast, something says no—
moving away so fast—nobody deserves that.

Ballentines. Because enough will never come and this won't go anywhere and today her bones hang dry and wrongly placed. Anyone sits with tightly crossed legs, torso curved over a nargilla pipe, an aura of sweet gray smoke drifting from him toward the dropping sun. Anyone smiles, up at her and she smiles back and the deep crack in her face stings as she walks through the glass doors. She hopes the room might swallow her whole, but the room holds only emptiness. The room couldn't be dimmer.

And with what happened with Y and the jeep, perhaps there should be less wandering out there. Best behind gates and doors, best to seal the cracks with towels, flip cable, argue over couch pillows, eat the last jar of Lebanese olives, lie about it, sink deep under Korean mink blankets, write letters to never send, throw the plastic soccer ball against every wall to the beat of Cat Stevens songs, drink mugs of vodka, smoke, smoke the nargilla, as the water gurgles gurgle back and bite at the smoke as the vodka settles, sketch out with thought—how to proceed with every new crack, how to plan with the bones building near the thinning surface, how to make Everyone recognize, the blocks and roads grow and that fine line between living as anything and nothing.

(Y has silent pupils, sadness, an arm in a taut, black sling, but her spine sits still and sober, her smell still skin lotion, Burberry clean. She says she might leave, and everyone nods, grunts agreements. She says she should probably stay.)

Calling from the Green Zone, his words choked in a bad connection.

I said I am flying into Erbil. Come meet me at the airport, it will be Newroz and I want to take you to my family.

The words, cut from air, arrive barely. She pushes back through the clog—

Okay, when?

Tomorrow comes the word out gagging.

Y says, yes, she's sure she should stay. The perfection of her straight spine and long fingers, placid and neat on her knee, her eyes don't leave the TV.

It's easier, it would be too much to explain. It would be too easy for everyone to say I told you so. *And the good thing about here is how easy we can hide.*

And everyone nods, grunts agreements.

It's called having nothing else to do, love, and I am sorry but this place was not made for jogging so no more of that, says O, appearing from the kitchen, a hand against each wall, a black olive in each eye socket.

Y mumbles something that sounds like *bon voyage*. She should ask her to repeat what she's saying, should keep the scene moving—ask how she did it, how she stayed so clean and smooth these last few months, ask who that was in her room and why they left so quick, ask what it was she wanted of them, ask what it was she got, ask what it feels like—yanked black in the arm by a stranger, running from a stranger, running from something so close, ask if she agrees that now it seems so clear what's possible, ask if she's proud and if she doesn't agree it's great to know it's possible to understand how far you can run, how quick you can run even when they're close behind—but it seems like so much work, such a heavy task to slow this moment down.

Airport: the first time she sees a bombing victim—a girl descending the steps of a plane with a windshield lined in fat red tape. Or, at least, she may be a bombing victim—given the face bubbled from chin to forehead, and the other passengers, the tangle of IVs, oxygen masks, the gauze peeking out of milk colored blankets. So many blankets.

The airport lobby warms with confusion, family and friends of the arriving and departing, pushing through the narrowness, corridors, the entrance, checkpoints and X-rays. Announcements come of cancellations, delays, overbooked flights and lost luggage.

She unknots, he's not there, realizes she had been knotted.

At the office, the editor-and-chief with one of his ideas: *You'll go away for the weekend—Newroz in the Rwanduz mountains—with AZ and his family. Make a story.*

Because Newroz can't be spent alone, AZ adds from the couch, half asleep. *It can't be spent anywhere but the tender green Rwanduz valleys and mountains.*

NEWROZ

A golden meadow grows in this story and out comes a king
who reigns with serpents sprouting from his shoulders.
He kills one boy a day, mashes down the brains to feed the
serpents, to alleviate the pain they leave in his shoulders.
Occasionally, out of either generosity or guilt, he mixes the
boy brain with a sheep's and cuts down on deaths. Spring
quits being green and warm while he reigns for those
thousands of years. (It's too long ago for anyone to really
know exactly how many years, or exactly how the story
played out.)

Calling now, from the airport three days late, he catches her in a garden shaped from cinder blocks, the coarse sound of roosters at her head, a girl with a name sounding something like *orphan*, rolls a toy truck across her feet.

Is that a rooster?

Yes, and a kid running me down with toys.

Yes, you really did leave the city, but I'm here. Where are you? I will come get you.

No more, she thinks. I'm sorry, she says.

(And a dark squeeze from the throat, her voice hardly through the slit.)

WHAT RWANDUZ CONSISTS OF

A proverb. In the springtime, animals and fatness; in the summertime, gardens and trees; in the wintertime, the fire and me.

(If only it was that simple.)

The art of fishing with grenades. She calls it cheating and AZ disagrees, chucking an explosive in the water, laughing, as the slick dead bellies of minnow-thin fish begin to pop and glint. It's small, less than a minute's burst of water, more contained than she'd have thought. But her ears vibrate, head oozes, torso splinters in death-panic—all expressed only through a disapproving shake of her head—a reaction AZ finds odd, funny, endearing.

Children. Like most in Kurdistan—Rwanduz houses are made of children. They carpet the floor and coat the walls.

This morning, the hovering breath of the girl with a name sounding something like *orphan* wakes her, hardly past 7, already aglow in hot pink sequins. Orphan needs her help— there's a picnic today, orange flowers to pin to her sleeve, there's things to be made perfect. *I love you*, says Orphan.

Those words. *I love you.* Loud at the doorway, soft at the cheek. These are the English words the women of AZ's family know best. These are the words they give her.

They love you, AZ confirms.

It's all they know how to say in English, she reminds him.

You shouldn't say that.

Sometimes, where I'm from, we say the words I love you not so much because we mean it, but because we need to hear the words get knocked around a bit.

But it's like you say at the office so much: All I know is what I have words for.

WHAT EXACTLY

Isn't clear, but she should say something. She doesn't quite have the words, though they hang nearby in the light of this valley, in the new grass edging the picnic rug, in the soft blue smoke of this bonfire, in this picking of small white flowers dotted along the road. Orphan sits on her lap, and the earthy smell from the nape of the child's neck leaves the American lonely, and a small leaf tugged from her coarse black curls only lonelier. Forget words, she decides. Rather something else come altogether—an utterance that, once heard, couldn't be misunderstood, forgotten, or knocked away. Like the sound of the world's population on their heads at once, the collective sound of rushing blood, lugging the pulse of seven billion hearts backwards to seven billion brains.

BECAUSE IT'S NICE TO THINK SOMETHING MIGHT TAKE

March ends, and the rain and heat begin. Again the air—hot and milky in the throat, buzzing the nostrils mad as insects, disrupting the path to the bakery, stunting patches of grass and weeds in concrete. Even the fig trees seem put out, and those sunflowers—those strange bursts of yellow from gray—planted again and sure to die. Though it's nice someone tried. Also, a newly planted Iraqi flag above the bazaar—tangled, wind knocking the green stars loose. And, again, the boy selling gum, swinging around the flagpole.

It's enough to crack her out of something she'd rather not climb back in, something here and yet to come, something that will remain long after she goes, something that will visit her at unexpected times—black as a pit, wandering sodden, lugging her pulse.

Back suddenly to tell her something, once the ouzo sinks in, the Man of Small Vital Facts starts first with windows shot out of the armored car leaving the Green Zone, the blown-up pet shop, the heat of it rising from neck to scalp.

I should have been dead many times. Why am I still here? But still I just laugh. I just laugh when I see my life almost fail before my eyes. You will either laugh or you will cry. That's it.

He laughs, so she laughs—a sling shot reaction, a hole through disconcertion and it's late, getting later and he hasn't yet said what he came here to say. It feels strange to see him, sudden and without time to decide if it leaves her happy. The throbbing once between her thighs stays long dead as it was when he left. In its place—just the smooth passing of uninterrupted minutes. Nothing erupts, no distractions down there and she has to work so early tomorrow.

(Later tonight, not long after she herself knows, she'll tell O and only O.

O sits picking the slivers of tobacco from the couch, another slug stain of cherry red setting in and responds, as though a punch line: Turns out he got engaged on Newroz! Someone he barely knows!

Did you think you could stop that? O, dissolving the red stain to blush with spit on her palm.

Did you think I wanted to?

Oh, please—there are plenty of reasons to not want to. There are always plenty of reasons but that never stops us. I've been witness to you looking at him, remember, love. And they always get engaged on Newroz.)

WHAT'S DONE

The newspaper offers a contract that would see her here
another year. Has her saying thanks but no, thanks but no
thanks to May's vapors and the dust fogging up a horizon
under construction, thanks but no, comes the mouth, I'm
afraid I cannot, out to the hidden foothills, thanks, but I'm
afraid I must decline, to the fractured face of an old mule
and those kids over there, bouncing dirty over roadside
petrol into sand bags, sending those empty plastic gas jugs
flying, thanks but, I'm afraid I must decline, thanks so much,
goodbye, *Xwahafez.*

WHAT WILL STAY

When the emails wane, first in length then frequency, carves, slowly, a cleave between now and what's absent. Like, the niece, E, her willowy fingers on sequins and lace, her demure mannered passion to kill all boys in Suleimania. And the questions she can never ask her: For how long will she keep her kill streak wishes? How many will she meet that feed it? Whom—if anyone—will she tell? What/who will shoot through her heart in return?

The child mechanic walks in front of the car as it idles at the checkpoint. Tree bark skin, ears poking from a heavy knit cap, a sober little man on his walk to work.

A tag with her name, originally attached to a fabric rose encased in a plastic tube found rolling around on the truck's back seat. *Because*, AZ says, *I knew you wouldn't stay.*

It makes sense, though, right? She asks.

As much as anything.

And how did you know?

Because I've never seen you do anything without thinking too much about it first.

WHAT'S GIVEN

She asks Max, One more story for the road?

If you put the spider's skin on a wound, it will stop the bleeding.

Good enough, sir.

XWAHAFEZ

A plane lands—a tired plane, blackened by exhaust, rust
edging the wings, the once serpentine emerald I's and A's
in the *Iraqi Airways* logo have dulled to stubs and a red tape
lines the wind shield.

That plane, out there, you see, yes?

A Jordanian businessman, shifts next to her in his steely gray
suit. Starch sounds come from his arms as he points at the
red taped plane.

Don't worry. Not ours! The shell of a seed snapping between
his incisors.

*Couldn't be. Those planes no leave Iraqi airspace. Not allowed because
they are not fixed enough! Those planes go from Baghdad and Basra, here
to Kurdistan only. South to North Iraq only. They bring the hurt here.
You know...boom-boom! Our plane will be chartered plane!*

She takes the offered handful of sunflower seeds. Pop and
crack, then crumbles of hard shards jab her gums, mild,
concealable tremors. She discreetly spits the seeds in a tissue,
sinking her teeth back in cheeks.

Good airline. Bad plane.

He continues, a one-way conversation, between words, starch
and pops. It's a welcomed distraction—his story about
Iraqi Airways. How the fleet's three planes were impounded
in the deserts of Jordan in 1990, during Iraq's invasion

of Kuwait. An effort to dodge embargo, destruction. The fleet's engineers in a warehouse, busied themselves only by assembling and disassembling a commercial jet engine, daily—a single flight simulator to keep the skills sharp, ensure their job would always stay possible.

True story? She asks.

They fly good, don't worry, but this is not our plane.

But he's wrong and the red taped plane is theirs. She boards last, the door a high pitch thump at her back, the engines buzz the carpet, vibrate the plastic cabin walls. It says she can't go back. A flight attendant signals her to the only vacant seat, a narrow place at the rear, right exit—a cabin crew seat. The flight attendant grins, removes a trash bag of bread rolls slumped in the seat, tosses it under an aluminum cart. He gestures—a wide sweep of the arm—to sit, then tucks himself in a crevice between the cart and divider, lights a cigarette.

In the initial climb toward home, on the first of too many flights, a jolt of turbulence pinches the gut, a clamp down of fear comes, so much fear and the pressured nerves lead to wonders: What would it feel and look like? Getting torn from this isolated pressurized bubble, to spill into magenta clouds and bumpy black air pockets. The seat gripped, slightly, teeth in cheeks, eyes nowhere much, blinking, while the whole world below goes on, suffocating and breathing, assembling and disassembling its innumerable pieces.

Acknowledgments

So many thanks to Bryan Tomasovich and Ewa Chrusciel for believing in this book; to those along the way who gave their attention to its many drafts: Leni Zumas, Joseph Crespo, Emily Crespo, Jamie Iredell, Lynda Majarian, Bronson Lemer, and Teddy Johnson; and to everyone I encountered and knew in Kurdistan—without whom this book would not be what it is, nor would this writer.

Emergency Press thanks Leah Rae Hunter, Frank Tomasovich, and Jill and Ernest Loesser for their generous support.

Emergency Press participates in the Green Press Initiative. The mission of the Green Press Initiative is to work with book and newspaper industry stakeholders to conserve natural resources, preserve endangered forests, reducd greenhouse gas emissions, and minimize impacts on indigenous communities.

Recent Books from Emergency Press

Gnarly Wounds, by Jayson Iwen

First Aide Medicine, by Nicholaus Patnaude

Farmer's Almanac, by Chris Fink

Stupid Children, by Lenore Zion

This Is What We Do, by Tom Hansen

Devangelical, by Erika Rae

Gentry, by Scott Zieher

Green Girl, by Kate Zambreno

Drive Me Out of My Mind, by Chad Faries

Strata, by Ewa Chrusciel

Various Men Who Knew Us as Girls, by Cris Mazza

Super, by Aaron Dietz

Slut Lullabies, by Gina Frangello

American Junkie, by Tom Hansen

EMERGENCY PRESS

emergencypress.org
info@emergencypress.org

Heather Rounds' poetry and short works of fiction have appeared in such places as *PANK*, *The Baltimore Review*, and *Big Lucks*. She's a co-founder of the roaming curatorial collective, The Rotating History Project, and currently lives in Baltimore.